This book is dedicated to every family that is
made, in ALL the ways families are made
—Ryan & Isaac

About This Book

The illustrations for this book were created digitally using Procreate and Adobe Photoshop Elements.
This book was edited by Farrin Jacobs and designed by Lynn El-Roeiy with art direction from Véronique Lefèvre
Sweet. The production was supervised by Virginia Lawther, and the production editor was Marisa Finkelstein.
The text was set in Ionic MT, and the display type is Filmotype Major.

Daddy & Dada

Hi, my name is Rumi.

Ryan Brockington & Isaac Webster

Illustrated by Lauren May

Little, Brown and Company

New York   Boston

I am four.
How old are you?

I have two dads.

Daddy sings songs with me.

Dada reads me stories.

They love me **THIS** much.

I have a baby brother named Xander.
You spell his name with an *X*, but it
sounds like a *Z*.

I like to make
him laugh.

He likes to pull
my hair.

I also have a dog. Her name is Betty.
She's very loud and very funny.

We're a family.
All five of us.

Daddy, Dada, Xander, Betty...and me.

Some of my friends have one dad and one mom.

Some of my friends
have one parent.

Daddy and Dada told me that families
come in all shapes and sizes.

Two dads.

One dad and one mom.

Two moms.

When we walk down the street, I see...

families of three,

families of four,

and families of five.

A boy in my neighborhood lives with
his grandma and her fluffy cat.

That makes a family of...three.

I know twins who have two dads and two brothers and three dogs!

That makes a family of...two plus two plus two plus three...nine!

Whoa. They have a big car.

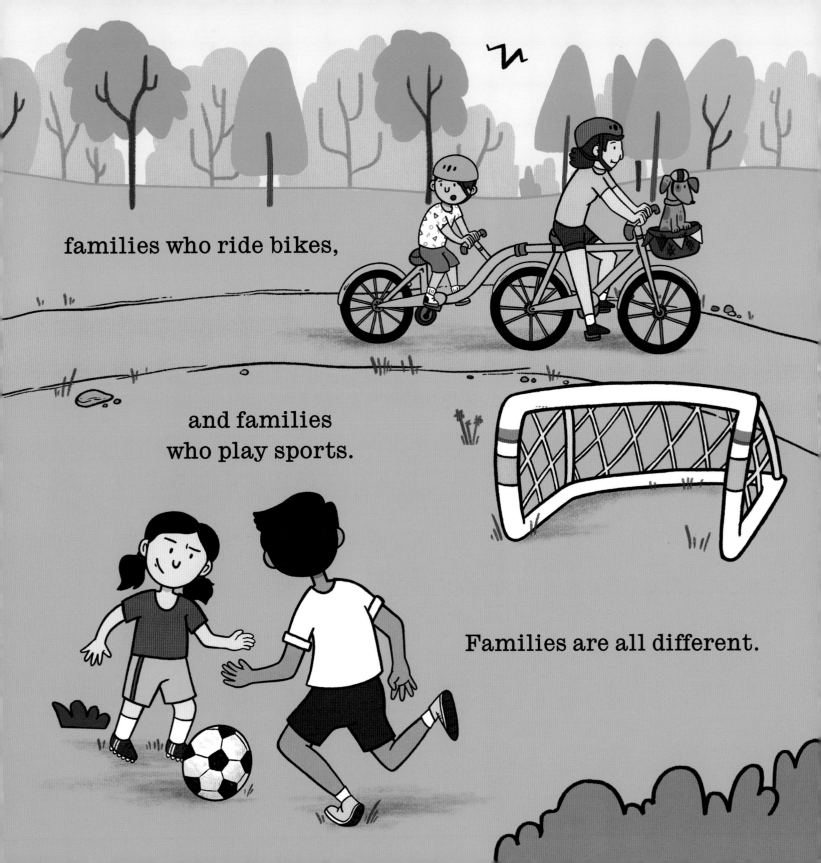

families who ride bikes,

and families who play sports.

Families are all different.

I also have two grandmas and two grandpas.

This is **Nan** and Pops.

This is Grammy and PaPa.

Plus there's Uncle TyTy
and Uncle RyRy.
I danced at their wedding,
and it was really fun.

And I love to visit
Aunt Katie, Uncle Jeremy,
and my cousins,
Ellie and Everett.

One of my friends calls me her sister.

And my dads say that's cool because sometimes
friends are just like family!

So, really, I have a lot of people in my family! Plus Betty!

This is us.

Daddy,

Dada,

Xander,

Betty, and me!

Tell me about your family.